By **Laurence Yep** Pictures by **Insu Lee**

AUNTIE TIGER

HarperCollinsPublishers

To Auntie Susie, who was always ready

to talk about movies with me

—L.Y.

For my mother, sister, Ross,

Jean, and Karen

—I.L.

Auntie Tiger

Text copyright © 2009 by Laurence Yep Illustrations copyright © 2009 by Insu Lee
Manufactured in China. All rights reserved.   No part of this book may be used or reproduced in
any manner whatsoever without written permission except in the case of brief quotations embodied
in critical articles and reviews. For information address HarperCollins Children's Books, a division
of HarperCollins Publishers, 1350 Avenue of the Americas, New York, NY 10019.
www.harpercollinschildrens.com

Library of Congress Cataloging-in-Publication Data
Yep, Laurence, date
  Auntie Tiger / by Laurence Yep ; illustrations by Insu Lee. — 1st ed.
    p.   cm.
  Summary: In this version of Red Riding Hood set in China, Big Sister sets aside her differences with
Little Sister to rescue her from a tiger in disguise.
  ISBN 978-0-06-029551-6 (trade bdg.) — ISBN 978-0-06-029552-3 (lib. bdg.)
  [1. Fairy tales.] I. Lee, Insu, ill. II. Title.
PZ8.Y46 Aun 2008   2006028649
[E]—dc22   CIP
                                                                                             AC

Typography by Jaime Morrell
1 2 3 4 5 6 7 8 9 10
❖
First Edition

A long time ago in China a widow lived deep in the woods with her two daughters. The younger sister was sweet but never did her chores, so the older sister had to do all the work.

"You're too lazy," the older sister scolded the younger.

"You're too bossy," the younger said to the older. And the two sisters fought as they always did.

Their mother would plead with them. "Big Sisters should take care of Little Sisters. And Little Sisters should listen to Big Sisters." But it never did any good.

One hot day their mother told them, "I hate to go into town because there's a terrible Tiger on the prowl. But we're all out of food. So don't open the door to anyone while I'm gone."

Now, who should be hiding in the woods but that very same Tiger, who had disguised himself as an old woman.

As soon as the mother left, the Tiger went to the house and growled, "My little dumplings, it's me, your Auntie."

However, Big Sister said, "My darling Auntie's voice is high, while yours is deep and gruff." And she wouldn't open the door.

So the Tiger gargled with some spring water. When he came back this time, he said in a high, high voice, "My little dumplings, it's me, your Auntie."

However, Big Sister peeked through the window. "My darling Auntie's hands are pale, and yours are orange and black." And she still wouldn't open the door.

So the Tiger covered his paws in flour. When he came back, he said again in his high, high voice, "My little dumplings, it's me, your Auntie."

Even when Big Sister saw how pale his paws were now, she did not want to let him in. "I'm sorry, my darling Auntie. Mother told us not to open the door to anyone."

"Oh, what a shame." Auntie Tiger sighed. "I've brought a special treat for my little dumplings."

Little Sister shoved Big Sister out of the way. "Quit bossing me. You can't keep the goodies—I mean, Auntie waiting." And she yanked open the door before Big Sister could stop her.

When Auntie Tiger stepped inside, Big Sister was still wary and wanted to see if he had a tail. "You look tired, my darling Auntie. Please sit down in this chair."

However, Auntie Tiger knew his tail would show. He said, "Wood is so hot, but porcelain is so cool. This big jar will be more comfortable than any old chair." He sat down with his tail dangling down inside the jar. But when he saw how plump and juicy the sisters were, his tail began to wag excitedly.

Thump-thump-thump, it went inside the jar.

"What's that noise, my darling Auntie?" Big Sister asked suspiciously.

"Mice," Auntie Tiger said quickly, and then yawned behind his paw. "Oh dear, this heat makes me feel so sleepy. I think I need to take a nap."

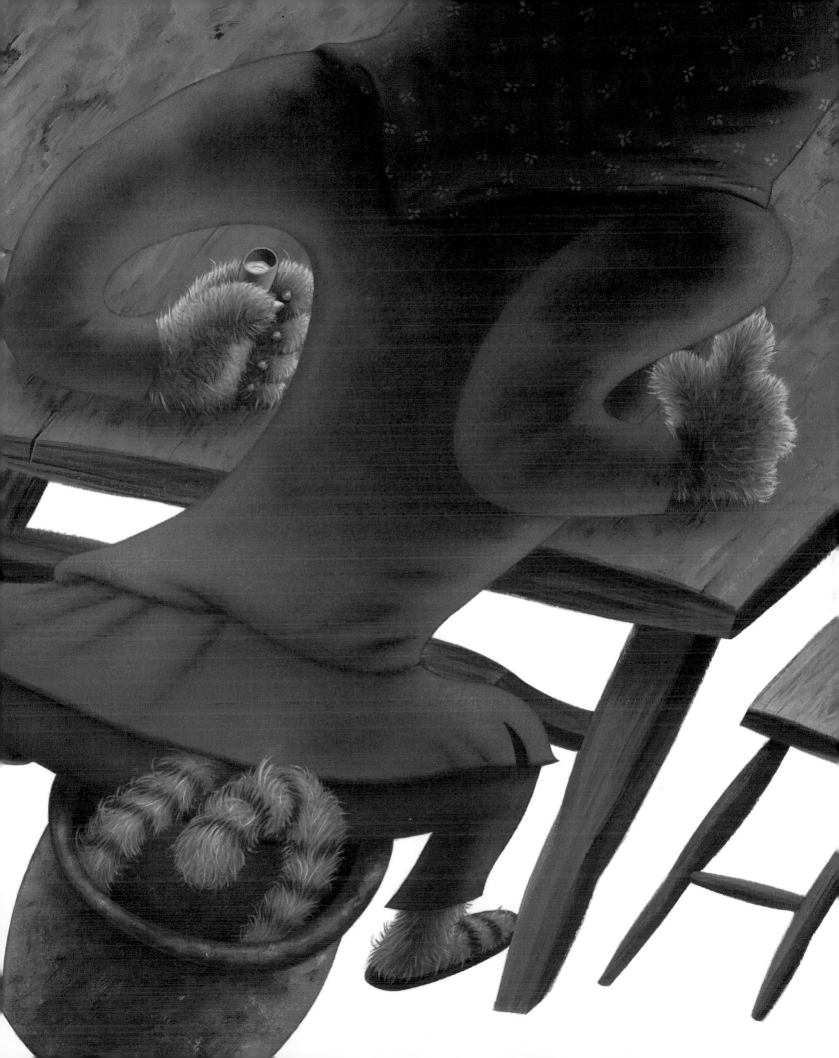

When the sisters led Auntie Tiger to their mother's bed, he mopped his forehead. "Oh dear, it's so hot. Won't one of you fan me while I lie down?"

Big Sister still didn't trust Auntie Tiger. "We have chores, my darling Auntie."

"The little dumpling who fans me can get out of them," Auntie Tiger coaxed. "And she'll get her treat first."

Little Sister jumped up and down. "Me, me, me!"

However, Big Sister was afraid to leave Little Sister alone with Auntie Tiger.

"My darling Auntie, you'll understand if we do our chores first."

Little Sister got mad at Big Sister. "You just don't want me to get the treat before you do." And she pushed Big Sister out of the room.

When Big Sister reluctantly went away, Auntie Tiger and Little Sister got into bed.

As she fanned Auntie Tiger, Little Sister asked, "Where's my treat, Auntie?"

Auntie Tiger crouched. "There's a big, fat, juicy dumpling . . . right here!" And he pounced.

Little Sister could have begged for her life, but all she could think of was Big Sister. "You were right, Big Sister," she tried to warn her.

She got no further because the Tiger gobbled her down whole.

Big Sister heard her and asked nervously,
"Little Sister, are you all right?"

But Little Sister couldn't answer anymore.

"Your sister is taking a nap," Auntie Tiger said sweetly.
"Why don't you come in and get your treat now."

Big Sister remembered her sister's warning, though.
"Auntie must be a Tiger," she said to herself. "My
poor little sister. Her last thought was to warn me.
She might have been lazy, but she was also very
sweet." Now that Little Sister was gone, Big Sister
realized how much she would miss her. "I was supposed
to protect her and I didn't."

She ran out of the house and climbed to the
top of a tall tree, where the branches were too
thin for the Tiger to go. And there she wept for
her lost sister.

Soon Auntie Tiger became impatient for the second course of his meal. He followed her scent straight to the tree.

"Come down, my little dumpling," Auntie Tiger called sweetly. "I have such a nice treat for you."

However, Big Sister was smarter than the Tiger. From her high perch, she called down, "And I have an even nicer treat for you, my darling Auntie. I found a whole nest of little birds up here. If you'll send up a bucket of water, I'll drown them for you."

Auntie Tiger smacked his lips greedily. "Yum, appetizers too." So he filled a bucket of water and brought it back. Then Big Sister lowered a rope and hauled the bucket of water up.

Auntie Tiger shouted, "My little dumpling, I'm getting
hungry. Are the birds ready yet?"

"Yes, darling Auntie," Big Sister lied, "but I'm afraid to
climb down the tree. Won't you bring me a bamboo pole
so I can slide down?"

So Auntie Tiger found a hollow bamboo pole behind
the house and brought it over to the tree. "Here, my little
dumpling. Now come on down."

"You know, my darling Auntie," Big Sister hinted, "I bet if I slid down, I'd go so fast I couldn't stop."

With a grin, Auntie Tiger stretched his jaw wide and set the bamboo pole inside his mouth so Big Sister would slide right into his belly.

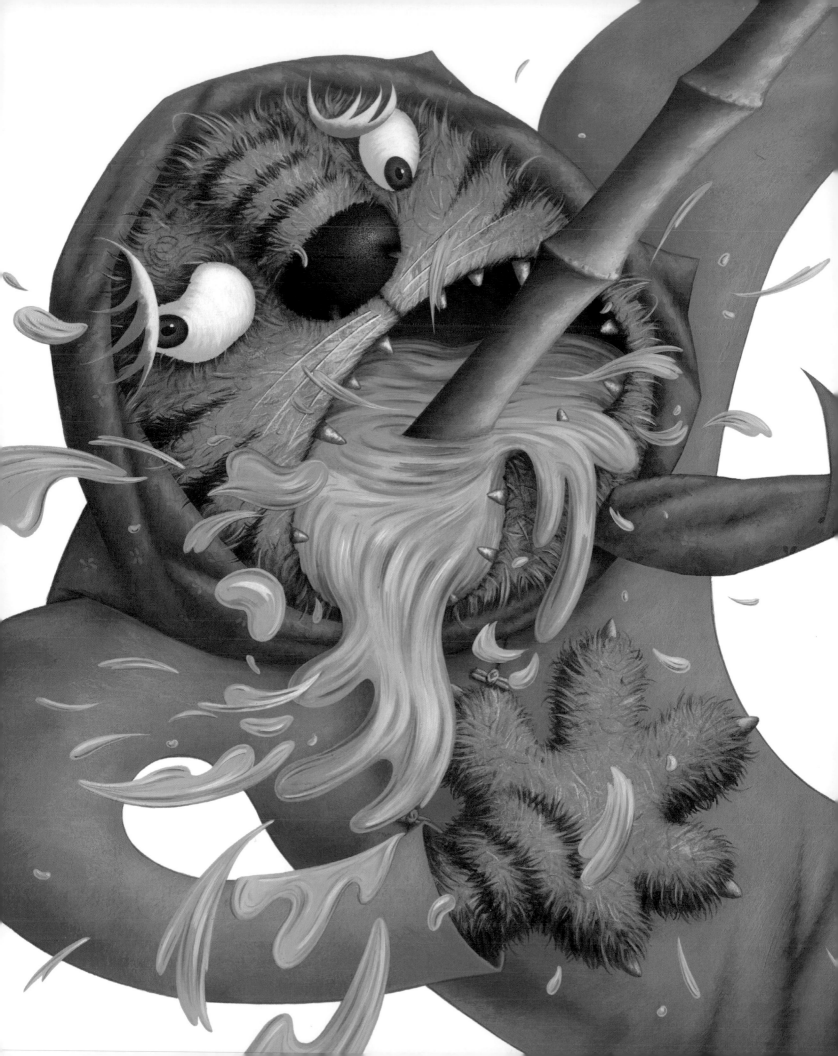

But Big Sister was peeking through the branches.
When she saw Auntie Tiger with the bamboo pole
in his mouth, she poured the bucket of water down
the hollow bamboo.

And the greedy Tiger drowned.

Then Big Sister got a knife from the kitchen and cut open the Tiger. And out stepped Little Sister, very wet but very much alive.

Little Sister gave Big Sister a hug. "I'll always listen to you, Big Sister."

"And I'll always take care of you," Big Sister promised.

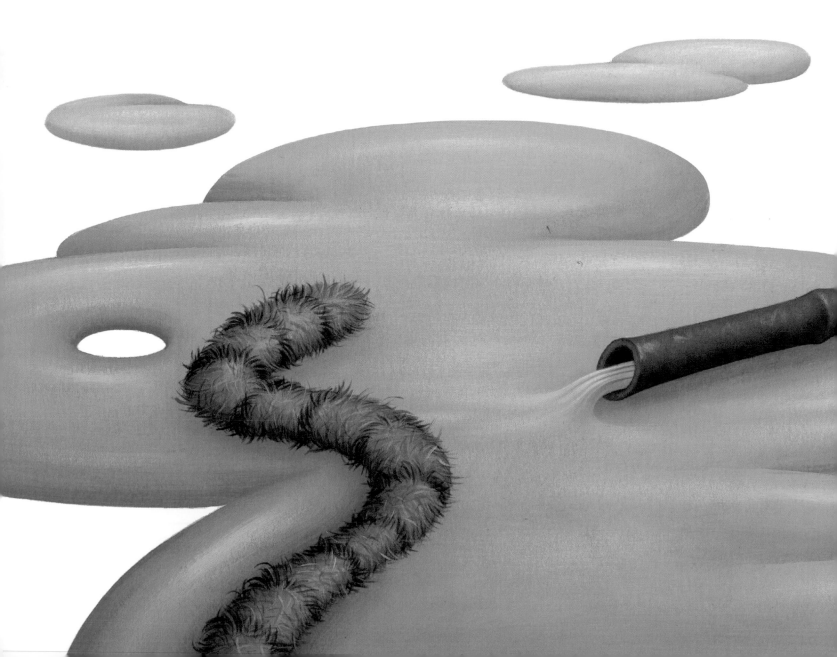

And when their mother came home with the food,
Little Sister took the basket from her.

"I'll heat up the dumplings," Big Sister said.

"And I'll make the tea," Little Sister said.

"No, you rest," Big Sister insisted.

Their mother blinked in surprise when she saw her
daughters working together so sweetly. "What's gotten
into you two? Are you really my girls?"

And over tea and dumplings, the sisters told their mother all about their visit from their darling Auntie Tiger and the special treat *they* had given him.